CANDY SPY

SIR PATRICK BIJOU

PRELUDE

While she's definitely sweet to look at, Agent Meg is more than just someone's arm candy... and she has an infinite number of successful missions to prove it.

As morning hits, Meg's eyes open to a sliver of sunshine behind 10-foot curtains. She's woken up in another bedroom. Again. This time, in South America.

Meg was tasked to smooch up a drug lord's son and retrieve an important package, which she did flawlessly. Of course.

All in a day's work of saving the world. Or, as Meg likes to call it, "another Tuesday".

Seducing dangerous men is part of her job as a spy for the Covert Analytical Network Design Yard a.k.a. CANDY. And with her looks and training, no one really stands a chance.

But she's really looking forward to a two-week vacation to Mykonos — the first break she's had in two years.

Working nonstop is all Meg can think about these days. However, much like anything in life, you can't always get what you want.

Meg finds this out the hard way: instead of packing a suitcase filled with bikinis, she's called to pack for a one-on-one with Director Bram Stoker — a child prodigy and her handler at CANDY.

A new mission is in the works as Meg needs to extract the "package" in one piece. However, this new mission is proving to be more trouble than Meg anticipated.

And if that's not difficult enough, she finds herself in the arms of a new lover... one she least expected.

*"**Candy Spy**" is a captivating action romance thriller for readers looking to live out their wildest adventures and fantasies. Overflowing with seduction, near-death confrontations, and titillating romantic encounters, readers are in for a roller coaster ride!*

ABOUT THE AUTHOR

Sir Patrick Bijou lives and writes from the United Kingdom and is the author of several books on finance and fiction. He is known for his extraordinary skills in settling and negotiating peace settlements and international law and is a prodigious legal and political adviser. His diverse writing ability has been influenced by many experiences, making him the success he is today.

Sir Patrick has written many books and articles about the liberation of people, highlighting the issues of those whom the literary world of creative writing has not enlightened. His expedition into content writing has made him a remarkably inspired author and professional communicator.

He has written over 40 non-fictional and fictional books spanning different genres.

Finding his Books.

To find out more about Sir Patrick, visit his website.

www.sirpatrickbijou.com
www.bijouebook.com

Men were such simple creatures. All you had to do was give them the hope of sex and they'd reveal their deepest secrets or surrender their most prized possessions. It was a tactic that had served Meg Brandon well, including last night - twice, if you wanted to be technical - when she ended up in bed with the son of South America's most corrupt politician. Luckily, he was handsome, rich, and correspondingly vain, so her mission was relatively easy. And surprisingly fun.

As she slipped out from under the gold-embossed covers, bathed in the narrow sliver of sunlight peeking through the ten-foot curtains, Meg was tempted to go for round three before bugging out. Wrinkling her nose at the naughty thought, she pressed a button on the side of her diamond-encrusted, titanium wristwatch. It produced a digital display over the traditional dials, revealing a countdown clock with only thirty-four minutes and eleven seconds left.

She'd misread the time earlier and thought she had at least an hour more. "Shit," she cursed under her breath, tiptoeing around the bed before reaching for her lacy, black bra tucked under her sleeping companion.

The mid-twenties man with shoulder-length brown hair and tanned skin jumped at the interruption, grabbing a shiny 9mm off the mahogany night stand. Seeing the half-naked woman standing in front of him in just frilly panties, he lowered the pistol's barrel and smiled. "You are going already?"

Damn, that was a wicked sexy accent and she definitely had a thing for dangerous men, but duty called. Bending down - and giving him an eyeful of the goods - she slowly licked her lips and smiled. "Oh, sweetheart. I wish I didn't have to, but I'm already late for work."

He grabbed her by the throat, the smile dropping into a suspicious glare. "Work? Who works on a Sunday?"

Not you, you arrogant little shit. All you do is mooch off daddy's dirty cartel money.

"An art dealer's job is never done," Meg replied coolly as wisps of her brown hair fell into her eyes, referring to her cover story instead of what she really wanted to say.

A few seconds passed as he searched her features for a hint of a lie, but her training was top-notch, and her nerves were made of steel. It would have been laughable to think this Latino playboy could break her when much better men tried and failed.

Seemingly satisfied with the answer, he pulled her closer into a rough kiss, pushing her away when he was done. Taking the cue, she began getting dressed, knowing he was watching every move.

"What was your name again?" he asked as she slipped the little black dress over hear head.

Meg straightened the hem of the skin-tight outfit, tugging at the bottom that stopped mid-thigh. "Does it really matter?" She bent down to pick up one of her discarded stilettos from the silk Persian rug before dropping to her knees to fish the second one out from under the bed.

Instead of answering, he threw the cover off himself, flung his legs over the side of the mattress, and stood up. Naked. Right there with everything at her eye- level.

Of course, she looked. Maybe even stared. Perhaps she could spare a few more minutes...

Focus, Meg told herself, clearing her throat before standing. "Thank you for your," she paused, touching her left earlobe to make sure her silver-and-sapphire, teardrop-shaped earring was still securely in place. "Your hospitality."

She turned to go, but he wrapped his fingers around her wrist and held her back. "It was my pleasure." The power-play may have worked on others, but she knew better than to engage. Standing still and silent, she looked at him with a perfect, innocent-doe expression until he let go.

After picking up her clutch from the ornate Louis IVX side table, she left the room and shut the door behind her. The burly bodyguard standing watch in an expensive suit and visible earpiece didn't give her a second thought as she hopped on one foot - and then the other - down the marble corridor while putting her shoes on. A houseful of cameras trailed Meg's every move as she descended the winding staircase and passed through the flower-filled entryway. The sweet smell of cut hydrangeas lingered in her nose as she exited the Italianate mansion and ran down the steps to the circular driveway.

A carved fountain with water spurting out of the mouths of three entangled dolphins - the tackiest thing she'd ever seen in her life - stood in the middle, surrounded by a row of high-end vehicles parked in succession. The engine of the silver, Tesla Roadster at the front roared to life, and the driver's side raised open as soon as she was in range.

Hopping into the custom leather seat, Meg pushed a comms button on the steering wheel while the door automatically closed. "Agent Finn, I'm going to need your help catching my flight."

She put the car into gear and peeled out, leaving a cloud of dust in the gravel.

"Copy, Agent Capulet. Do you have the package?" A male voice with an English accent replied over the secure communications channel.

"Affirmative," Meg said, flying down the private access road leading away from the estate. "Now get me out of here before they realize I took it."

"I'm pulling up the quickest route for you right now," Finn replied before a digital map appeared on the built-in screen in the center of the dashboard.

Meg glanced at the display, orienting herself with the blinking spot indicating her present location against the winding, blue line leading to the airport across town. She looked up just in time to see a tractor pulling onto the road, and she yanked the wheel sharply to the left to avoid a collision.

"Are you all right?" Finn asked. "I noticed a sudden spike in your heart rate. I ignored the readouts last night for obvious reasons, but now that you're on the road--"

"Yes, I'm fine," she snapped, internally cursing herself for letting the Yard implant her with a bio-tracker microchip. Even an international spy needed occasional privacy, even if she was fooling around on work-time with a high-profile target.

She had less than a mile of uninhibited road before coming up to the end of a long queue of cars stopped at a red light. Meg tapped her French-tipped nails on the wheel. "I'm going to need you to do your magic on the traffic signals."

"On it." The affirmation came immediately.

She sighed, looking for a possible way around the gridlock. There was none. A few seconds later, the light turned green and the cars began to move. With a racing driver's precision, Meg skillfully cut in front of a maroon Honda on the right, floored the accelerator,

then weaved in front of a black Jeep. As expected, the next light gave the go-signal as well, and so did all of the others she came across, even after turning right three blocks later.

Agent Finn was a gem.

"How much time do I have left?" She continued to speed through the city traffic under the shadows of giant swaying palms.

"Twenty-three minutes."

Not even she could manage to make that. "Stall the plane, Agent Finn. Nothing extreme. Just a false little mechanical error report that can be resolved in just enough time for me to make it there."

There was a brief pause before he answered. "I need additional clearance for that."

"Well, get the damn clearance!" she yelled.

"Copy. I'll be with you in a sec." He went off-line, temporarily leaving her alone.

Of course, she wasn't totally alone. Agent Huck Finn - obviously not his real name, but an alias given to an operations support technician at the Covert Analytical Network Design Yard - was just Meg's remote wingman out in the field. A whole slew of analysts back at headquarters - and probably in other top secret, redundant back-up locations, as well - could also track her whereabouts, listen to their conversations, and provide assistance as soon as she asked for it. But as a senior CANDY agent, Meg had a lot of discretion on how she ran her ops. Only her handler, Director Stoker, could override her.

"Agent Capulet?" Finn came back on the line just as she merged onto a four-lane highway, heading toward the' Aeropuerto'.

Meg crossed three lanes and floored the gas pedal. "Copy."

"I was just informed that flight 793 heading to Washington has been delayed due to an inexplicable spike in tire pressure during the pre-departure check," he said with a slight hint of amusement in his voice.

She laughed. "Well done." She sped along for another half mile, passing an increasing number of orange, diamond-shaped signs. "The GPS is showing me to take the next exit, but there seems to be road construction up ahead."

"So . . . that shouldn't be there." Finn's tone was hesitant, maybe even unsure.

The reply didn't quell Meg's growing unease. "Pull up a live satellite feed and give me an alternate route, stat."

"Yes, ma'am," he said, becoming uncharacteristically formal.

Shit. Thorough prep was key to a successful mission. Any time something unexpected happened, things went bad.

"My exit is blocked. I repeat, my exit is blocked. I need an alternative route, NOW!" Meg demanded as she flew past the barricaded road that would have taken her to the airport's cargo entrance.

"In two hundred feet, there'll be a restricted access road on your left for emergency vehicles only. Make a U-turn there and take the first exit off the highway," Finn instructed with his usual confidence. "Go left at the overpass, then straight for another mile."

With no other options, Meg followed the directions. Soon she was passing a chain link fence and could see the end of the runway beyond.

"Gate C is ready for you," the agent on the end of the line said. "One hundred fifty feet on the right. No need to slow down; the way has been cleared."

"Finally, some good news," she replied, seeing the small security booth flanking the open gate. Slowing just enough to take the ninety-degree turn without hitting the uniformed guard standing at its entrance, the Tesla's tires screeched as it fishtailed before driving onto airport territory. "Where's the plane, Finn?"

Meg dodged a catering truck and then overtook a baggage trailer before cutting across under the wing of a parked plane.

"Off-gate outside Terminal 2 to your left. It's the only A330 on the tarmac in the immediate vicinity, so you can't miss it. Just watch out for the --"

"Firehoses?" She finished the sentence as her car was doused in water. Turning on the windshield wipers, she frowned. "Yeah, found those."

"Sorry about that. I should have mentioned you were in the plane wash area." Finn laughed. "It means you're close. Do you have visual?"

"Affirmative," she said, coming up on the waiting aircraft. A man in an orange vest was ready for her, signaling directions to park in front of an adjacent cargo loader. "Thanks for your help, Finn. Agent Capulet is signing off."

Pressing the' valet mode' button before opening the door, she swung her legs over the threshold and got out. "Try not to scratch it. I just had it washed," she instructed the befuddled looking baggage handler, who probably didn't know what to ogle harder: the exotic car or the beautiful woman driving it.

She retrieved a carry-on from the trunk and handed her boarding pass - pre-printed thanks to Agent Finn - to the flight attendant at the bottom of the mobile stairs.

"It is a pleasure to have you on board with us today, madam." The woman smiled before ushering her to a first-class seat.

When her car had been loaded, and the cabin doors were secured for take-off, Meg sat back and sipped chilled champagne in a solo-salute to having another job completed. Tomorrow she'd hand off the package to Stoker and start her well-deserved vacation. Two weeks on Mykonos wouldn't make up for having continuously worked for the last two years without a break, but at least it was something.

By the time the plane reached its cruising altitude, however, a text from the Yard quickly spoiled her outlook: Monday 0800. YTS2. Keep your bags packed.

Meg could disarm the timing mechanism on a plutonium bomb in under three minutes with just gum, tweezers, and a nail file, but for some reason, she always had trouble finding the right key to lock her apartment door. After rummaging through the bottom of her blue Kate Spade handbag, hoping the third time would be the charm, she pulled out a chain attached on one end to a silver key and a dangleyboop in the shape of a pirate's skull and crossbones on the other.

"Finally," she huffed, sticking the key into the lock while pulling the doorknob toward her. After turning the contraption until she could hear the click of the deadbolt, she spun around to leave but didn't make it two paces before her neighbor's door opened.

"Good morning," the handsome-in-that-nerdy-kind- of-way man said as he stepped out. A mix of Clark Kent and Harry Potter, he'd moved in two years ago, just a few weeks after her. They often left for work at the same time, but in spite of their similarities in age and apparent marital status - chronically single and loving it, thank you very much - they never found much other common ground. For Meg, it was just as well. In her line of work, friends would be a distraction and a liability. Not only would she have to find believable stories to cover up why she was gone so often (the truth was not an option), but anyone close to her could always become a target.

Although she tried to keep her neighbors at arm's length, apparently, this one was a pro at locking doors. He was done and next to her before she could slip away. Wearing a charcoal gray suit, tortoiseshell glasses, and a striped tie, he also had the typical K Street look. Luckily, he was one of the few remaining good guys, lobbying for something that actually mattered.

"Hey, Ryan." Meg returned the greeting as they began to walk side-by-side down the hallway to the stairs. "How's saving the birds going lately?"

"We've made some real progress in pushing through new legislation to expand protection for the jack pine warbler," he said with way too much enthusiasm for seven am.

She smiled. "Today the warbler, tomorrow world peace."

"I'll do my best." He chuckled as they took the first step down.

Continuing in silence for the duration of the three flights, they only spoke again when they'd walked through the lobby and out of the building's glass front door.

"Have a great day," Ryan said, turning left on the sidewalk.

Meg turned right. "Thanks. You, too."

She walked a few blocks before taking the escalator down to the Metro platform. An orange line train had just pulled out from the station, but a blue train was directly behind. The car was already packed, but the throng of commuters pushed their way on board. Squeezed between a teen in a charter school uniform carrying an enormous backpack and a graying man with a buzz cut in a dark blue suit, Meg steadied herself by holding on to the overhead grab bar. A family of four in shorts, tees, and sneakers - the go-to outfit for most out-of-town tourists - sat across the aisle perusing a local guidebook while two women in hijabs chatted in French behind them.

Mornings in DC were both mundane and extraordinary. No other city in the world was as full of diversity and political power, yet still experienced the simple frustrations of getting to work on time while maintaining your cool.

Today, that applied both figuratively and literally. The train car's AC couldn't keep up with the combination of summer heat and overpacked conditions, and Meg

could feel the silk blouse under her fitted jacket stick to her body. She frowned. How in the world did technology exist to grow a human ear on the back of a mouse, but a breathable fabric couldn't be tailored into a professional garment?

At least the trains ran consistently, which was a win. When they pulled up to the Federal Center stop a few stations later, Meg pushed her way out of the car and made a beeline to the escalator. She was still four blocks from her destination, but her route was through the blocky, concrete federal property built in the 1940s, located right outside the exit.

The FBI once used the six-story Ford Building, and it currently held the offices of the US House of Representatives. Pulling a laminated ID badge out of her purse and throwing the lanyard around her neck, Meg took the marble steps as fast as her heels and pencil skirt allowed. In the lobby, she joined a short queue for a security check. After scanning her bag and passing through a metal detector, she headed toward a group of elevators in a nearby - yet inauspicious - corridor.

Meg pressed the call button for "DOWN," and although two of the four elevators opened soon thereafter, she waited for the last one on the left to become available. She stepped inside, but another woman entered before the doors closed.

"Oh, I thought this was going down." The woman - about her age with blonde hair in a tight bun - looked at the panel of available floor numbers. Starting at L stands for lobby at the bottom, the round buttons went upward numerically until six.

Meg had been holding the door "OPEN" button to keep the elevator from leaving. "You'll have to take one of the other three, I'm afraid. This one is special."

"Oh, I never realized. Thanks," the woman replied before getting out.

Meg waited for the doors to slide closed before opening a panel labeled "Emergency Phone."

Removing the handset, she waved her ID in front of a nearly indiscernible red light in the recess. The light turned green, and she pressed a six-digit code on the phone's keypad. As soon as she returned the phone to its place, the elevator began its descent into the secret underbelly of the nation's capital that not even its Congressmen knew about.

Five stories down - three below the lowest level most people in this building ever went - Meg stepped out of the elevator. After a small landing, a stairwell of exactly thirty steps with an arched ceiling lined with yellowing subway tiles led further down. At the bottom, a seemingly forgotten, nineteenth-century subway station stood empty. Its ribbed vaults were topped with faux skylights of stained glass, hidden illumination simulating the natural sunlight that couldn't possibly be real more than one hundred feet below the surface.

A slight movement in the air and the low hum of machinery signaled the approach of her ride, and within seconds, a futuristic people-mover pulled up. Comprised of a single car that contained only four seats - two on opposite ends facing each other — its clean lines, white color, and modern technology were in stark contrast to the rest of the surroundings.

Meg got on, but like with everything else, after she input her access code in the elevator, the ride was automatic. The machine knew where to deliver her, and after zooming through a criss-cross of pitch-black tunnels for less than a minute, it came to a smooth stop.

"Welcome to CANDY, Agent Capulet," a robotic voice greeted her as she stepped onto the platform. Unlike her departure station, the aesthetic here was less Augustus Pugin and more Steve Jobs. Carved into the bedrock under Washington, DC, everything that wasn't glass or concrete was pure white. And here, she was immediately in the center of the activity.

Men and women wearing dark suits and holding clipboards or file folders hurried back and forth, often disappearing down adjacent hallways or into glass-walled meeting rooms. The thirty-foot ceilings allowed an open catwalk connecting several suspended offices, fully utilizing the unusual space.

With nearly ten minutes to spare, Meg took the long way to the director's office. A logistics coordinator - Agent Orsino, wasn't it? - caught her as she passed the infosec unit.

"His schedule's changed, so Director Stoker wants to see you immediately." The older man handed her a mug. Wisps of steam were still rising from the top. "Fat free milk, no sugar, right?"

Taking the coffee, she smiled. "Yes. Thanks."

The beverage was just cool enough to sip by the time she stopped in front of a frosted-glass door. Moving the mug away from her lips to allow the faint laser beam to scan her facial features, she waited for the door to slide open before entering.

The director was standing across the room with his back to her, studying a map of north Africa projected onto the wall. He waited for the door to close and hermetically sealed off the space before speaking. "Morning, Megara," he addressed her by her full, legal name, preferring the convention over aliases when meeting his agents privately.

"Good morning, sir," she replied, walking closer. "Are you planning on sending me to the Sahara?" she jokingly guessed.

Stoker turned, but there wasn't a hint of amusement on his young face. And young definitely wasn't an understatement. Standing in his custom-made suit, skinny black tie, and sun-bleached (and perhaps a bit over-gelled) hair, Meg still had to tell herself to remember to take her boss seriously, even if he was seven years old junior. And she was only twenty-five!

Director Bram Stoker may have been a child prodigy but wasn't an anomaly at CANDY. Many potential agents were recruited in their late-teens and trained to be super-spies. Hell, her start at the Yard a year out of college practically made her a late-bloomer! But he had gotten fast-tracked to a supervisory role as an unmatched computer hacker and equally talented criminal profiler. And he had proven to be damned good at the job, having fifteen successful missions in the last two years with just her alone.

Thanks to protocol, Meg didn't even know the cover identities of the others under Stoker, but one piece of information was common knowledge: he hadn't lost an agent yet. So, in spite of her fatigue - she'd only gotten home from South America late last night - she knew to trust him to make the right call if the welfare of the nation depended on it.

Stoker took a step forward and held out his palm. "I trust you have the package?"

Meg put her coffee down before reaching for her right earlobe. She removed the earring and handed the gem-encrusted tear drop jewelry over. "You were right about the weakness in their encryption algorithm. It was almost laughably easy to get to the data."

"Of course, I was right," he muttered, retreating behind a console holding three flat-screen monitors. The earring easily snapped into a specially designed case that converted it into a flash drive, which Stoker inserted into the accompanying computer. Within seconds, he had access to the information Meg had copied off her target's cell phone.

"Is it what you had hoped to get?" she asked, picking her mug up again before taking a sip.

Without taking his eyes off what was displayed on the screens, he nodded. "It'll take some time to scrub this intel, but yes, I think it'll prove useful."

She didn't prod further. Her job was to get information. What that information was, what it meant, and what it could do (and who it could do it for) wasn't her concern.

Meg took another gulp of coffee, the smell of the dark roast lingering in her nostrils. "Your message yesterday said something about not bothering to unpack, sir?"

He looked around the monitor. "You know I didn't mean that literally, right?" The first hint of teenage self-doubt emerged. Getting up, Stoker rounded the desk then leaned back against it, extending his long legs and crossing his ankles. "Obviously, you should take some clean clothes."

"Of course, sir." Meg had to hold back a smile. "And what is my destination?"

"You'll be on an afternoon flight to Skopje for a quick recon mission. It shouldn't take more than a few days," he said. "My understanding is you had plans to vacation in Greece?"

She nodded. Drinking ouzo under a beach umbrella in the near future seemed less and less likely.

Stoker crossed his arms. "If you'd like, we can deliver an extra bag to your hotel there. Macedonia is just across the border. You can go on your holidays as soon as you're done."

Suddenly, Meg could feel the warm sand under her toes. "That would be perfect. Thank you, sir. And what kind of information will I be looking for?"

"SAL will brief you. She's waiting for you upstairs when you're ready."

James Bond's MI-6 had Q, the Kingsmen had Merlin, and CANDY had SAL. A funny, intelligent, and dependable thirty-something year old who led the Yard's gadget lab, they were also Meg's favorite coworker after Agent Finn. Too bad they were just a hologram.

A holographic interface for artificial intelligence focused on Strategic Adaptive Learning - SAL - to be precise. The name denoted that the longer they existed, the smarter they became. And smart was an understatement. SAL could create a fabric that would tell whether its wearer was lying based on the content of their sweat and develop a type of sign language using just a series of nods to communicate with cats, all before breakfast. Well, before what would be breakfast time, if they had needed to eat.

Recently, they had designed Meg's micro-storage unit that held 2 terabytes of data without employing any traditional circuitry, all while looking like $100K worth of earrings. Meg couldn't wait to see what new toys they'd come up with next.

After taking the paternoster - a strange but effective contraption that was a cross between a ladder and an elevator - up to the catwalk, Meg walked across the all-glass hallway and entered the innovation lab. It was a circular room with a large, similarly-shaped table in its center and a great view of the people-mover station below. But Meg was more interested in what was happening right in front of her.

The table's surface had a three-foot diameter circle cut in its center. This was where SAL existed in their visual form, with perfectly proportionate arms and legs, perfectly done hair and makeup, and perfectly pleasant demeanor and attitude. In short, SAL was perfect. If they hadn't been slightly see-through, they would have been considered the perfect specimen humanity had ever produced. This was especially true now as they stood in front of Meg, posing seductively in nothing but a white bustier, garter belt, and g-string.

"Uh, honey, did you forget to get dressed this morning?" Meg asked with a smile, shutting the door behind her.

"I am fully dressed for our purposes, Agent Capulet," SAL replied. "I have been anxious to show you my latest invention."

Meg let out a small sigh, relieved that the virtual brains behind the operation 'weren't losing their digital marbles. "You have a set of those for me?"

She stopped at the table's edge. Almost immediately, a panel opened on the apparently seamless, shiny black surface, and an unseen mechanism lifted a gift box holding an identical set of undergarments.

"34-26-34, I believe, is your size." SAL smiled as Meg took the items.

Meg held the bustier against her torso. "What does it do?"

"Besides, make anyone who sees you in them want to rip them right off?" The hologram flipped their platinum-blonde hair over their shoulder.

"You know me too well, SAL." Meg turned the clothing over, trying to discover any hint of its uniqueness. She found none. "But I assume these aren't something anyone could pick up at Victoria's Secret?"

"That is correct. Allow me to demonstrate." SAL vanished, and a miniature projection of a mid-rise building appeared in their place. Although unseen, they were always present, and their voice continued to ring throughout the room. "Imagine that you are caught in a situation that requires a quick exit."

Meg instinctively nodded, recalling several instances where the speed of her getaway saved her life. As SAL zoomed in on a tenth-floor balcony, the agent shifted her position around the table to get a better view.

"The regular routes are blocked. No elevator. No stairs." SAL created an equally tiny version of themselves on the small exterior ledge. They were

gripping the railing and looking down into the nearly one-hundred-foot drop. "The only way is down."

"All right," Meg said, still not understanding how lingerie was going to save her.

"But you are wearing these." SAL drew their hands down their body, modeling the garments before throwing their slender leg over the metal bar. "So, you can calmly climb out like so and jump."

Meg's eyes widened as she watched the six-inch hologram swan dive off the ten-story balcony. Like in a movie where the director went from a tight, close-up to a wider frame, the display pulled back. The building could be seen in its entirety, but mini-SAL was still plummeting toward the surface. Everything occurred so fast, Meg didn't even have time to begin to worry because about a third of the way down, a parachute - thin as fog but obviously doing its job - popped open and safely delivered SAL to the ground.

As soon as their feet touched the grass below, SAL became their previous five-foot eight-inch self again.

Turning their back to Meg, they pointed to the section of the bustier between their shoulder blades. "The compressed pouch holding my ultra-thin fabric is there, but you'll find that it doesn't diminish the garment's comfort."

"Wow," Meg whispered, still amazed by what she'd just seen.

"You will need to manually cut the tethers." SAL faced her, holding a switchblade. Reaching behind their neck, they gathered the thin cords holding up the parachute and severed them swiftly. "For now, this system is for one-time use only."

"Gotcha. Anything else?" Meg asked, her excitement growing at the thought of trying out the goods.

SAL's image vibrated, and they reappeared fully dressed in a dark gray suit and their hair now closely shorn. "The deployment mechanism is automatically triggered, so need for you to calculate range or speed. However, it won't know the difference between situations, so I would highly advise against wearing this on a roller coaster."

Meg couldn't help but snicker at the mental image. "No problem." Sensing that she'd heard everything about her new gadget, she put the lingerie back in the box and pulled up a chair. "Stoker's sending me to Macedonia. Do you want to tell me why?"

Making a holographic map appear, SAL smiled. "Oh, you're going to like this."

"I don't think I've ever said I preferred any of my previous assignments over the other, so why would you think I would be especially excited about this one?" Meg asked.

"I assumed because twenty-three percent of your online browsing history is somehow related to celebrity gossip, you'd enjoy a mission that involves the creme de la creme of international celebrity: royalty." SAL drew out the final word in a breathy tone, making the reveal the same way a game show host would introduce a grand prize.

Although Meg was intrigued, she was also a little creeped out that not only was SAL Internet stalking her, but also coming to such logical conclusions. "Royalty?"

"That is correct." SAL nodded before pointing at the digital map projected behind them. "Are you familiar with the Sovereign Principality of Luxenstein?"

"The barely twenty square-mile city-state in northern Europe under the governance of an immensely wealthy family that can trace its roots back to 16th century Prussia? Who isn't?" Meg deadpanned before flashing a coy smile.

SAL was not amused, continuing on with their briefing in complete seriousness. "Two years ago, the Grand Duchess who ruled the principality died under - what some would call - mysterious circumstances. Already a widow at the time of her death, the logical choice in succession was her twenty-three-year-old son Henri Thibaud von Alsace-Thuringen."

A photograph of the man in question replaced the map. Chiseled jaw, straw-yellow hair, and wearing a military uniform with a bright blue sash and lots of shiny medals, he was the quintessential picture of the fairytale Prince Charming. "Wow." Meg inadvertently mouthed a surprised exclamation. SAL was correct; this mission was right up her alley.

"Henri was never crowned, however," the hologram said as another picture appeared next to one of the heirs. The man in this was equally good-looking and about the same age but with dark hair and a less jovial demeanor. "A long-lost 'cousin' showed up in Luxenstein three days before the ceremony, putting in an official claim to the title, lands, and fortune. The issue is still with the lawyers and has not been settled to this day."

"How am I supposed to unmask a pretender?" Meg's thoughts quickly shifted from wondering what it would be like to waltz around the ballroom of a real palace to how to get the blonde hottie his royal inheritance.

"Oh, Wiktor Liebchenko isn't a pretender. My analysis of the documents he's provided to the High Court shows that his paternal great-grandmother was the youngest sister of Henri's great uncle, former Grand Duke Alexander." SAL scrolled through a virtual tablet computer that materialized in their digital hands as if they were reviewing the papers a second time. "His case has legitimacy."

Losing her patience at the seemingly extraneous information, Meg raised her palms and shrugged. "What does all of this have to do with my mission, then? And why are we even discussing Luxenstein when Stoker sends me to Macedonia?"

SAL looked up from the screen. "Henri's sister has been kidnapped," they said.

"Oh," Meg whispered. Things just got interesting. Maybe this Wiktor character was tired of waiting on a judicial decision and wanted to force Henri's abdication through blackmail. "Go on."

"Astrid Louisa von Alsace-Thuringen was last seen Saturday afternoon touring the Paris opera house where her eighteenth birthday celebrations were to take place in two weeks. After leaving the Palais Garnier, her chauffeured Mercedes was captured on CCTV camera entering this tunnel on the north side of the Seine River at half past three." A video of the event appeared next to SAL, showing a succession of cars speeding down a two-lane road flanking the water.

The image paused on a dark sedan. "This is Astrid's vehicle. We do not indicate that she left it between when she got in and when this was taken. Note that the tunnel is only fifty yards long. At this speed, it can be traversed in a few seconds. See the time stamp and this white carrier van behind it?"

Meg nodded, sensing the importance of those particular pieces of information. When the image changed to cars leaving the tunnel just three seconds later, she looked for the van. It was there, but the Mercedes in front of it was gone.

SAL sped up the video, stopping it twenty-two minutes later according to the new timestamps. "This

is when Astrid's car finally emerged from the tunnel. The driver headed to Le Grand Hotel where Astrid had been staying, entered her suite using her key card, and was promptly shot in the back of the head by an unknown assailant."

"Are we assuming she changed vehicles in the tunnel and left with someone else?" Meg asked, tackling one issue at a time. A dead driver was secondary to a kidnapped Duchess.

"Yes. And based on local law enforcement follow-ups, we believe it was here." SAL rewound the video to just a few minutes after the van emerged, focusing on a motorcycle with two people on board. "This Ducati only had one rider when it entered the tunnel."

"Why didn't they use a car? Stick her in the trunk, or at least have her huddle in the back? Why make it so obvious?" Every indication pointed to Astrid leaving willingly, yet why murder the driver and not just take him along?

"That is one thing you'll need to find out in Skopje." SAL made the video disappear. "After following the vehicle registration, the trail led to a real estate developer in Macedonia."

Meg sighed and crossed her arms. This sounded like a complicated case. It definitely couldn't be cracked in two days. "Do you think she's there?"

SAL shook their head. "It's unlikely. And a ransom hasn't been demanded, nor has there been any type of effort to contact the Alsace-Thuringen family. But Director Stoker does think there's some connection, so you'll need to go and find out whatever you can that will help get us started."

"You'll have my usual documents ready before I leave today?" Meg asked, referring to her fake passport, flight tickets, and foreign currency.

"We're assembling them now," SAL said. "How much longer will you be in the building?"

Meg sighed. She was desperate for sleep but was also scheduled for a training session before meeting her mother for lunch. "Another hour?" she guessed before standing.

SAL nodded. "That should be adequate. Oh, and Agent Capulet?"

"Yes?"

The holographic image virtually tapped the table in front of them. "Don't forget to leave the other earring."

Meg left SAL's office and headed one more level down. As a field agent, she didn't have clearance to enter most of the rooms reserved for surveillance and data analysis, but she did gain admittance to the workout facilities. After changing into spandex pants and a sports bra, she entered the gym. Like with everything else at CANDY, it was super futuristic, and for the next hour, it was reserved just for her and Wilson Yi.

Wilson was the only CANDY agent she knew who didn't have a code name. No one ever said why, and she always felt super awkward asking, so it was one of those things that remained unsaid. He was also surprisingly open about his early life growing up in Hong Kong, joining the British

Special Forces as an eager twenty-year old, and finally getting recruited by the Yard. That was more than two decades ago, and every time Meg saw his amazingly buff physique, she had to remind herself that Wilson was over twice her age.

There was the saying' black don't crack' (seriously, what was Halle Berry's secret?), and Meg really needed to find out what the equivalent was for Asians because - that's right - Wilson was fifty.

Mind. Blown.

Of course, knowing how much time he spent training and the skills he used to whip agents into shape explained the discrepancy between what she saw and the incredible birthday math. Still, Meg's pulse always quickened just a bit when she stepped into Wilson's sanctum, and today was no different. It also didn't hurt that he liked to work out half-naked, giving a great view of his ripped upper body.

"Agent Capulet," he greeted her, walking up in just basketball shorts and giving her a European kiss of a peck on each cheek. "Just in time."

"I'm rather jet-lagged, and I'm off again tomorrow, so I'm afraid we'll have to have a shorter than usual session today," she said, trying her best not to ogle his rock-hard pecs in the dimly lit space. Windowless - like everything else at CANDY - it looked more like the interior of a spaceship than an underground training room with its shiny, dark surfaces and blue fluorescent lights.

"Well, then, let's not waste another moment." Wilson smiled, brushing his jet-black hair from his forehead and pointing to two mats on the floor nearby. "Let's start with a bit of yoga, shall we?"

They quickly went through some warm-up poses before taking on more expert-level stretching exercises. Starting with the Side Crane pose, they focused on creating a strong central axis. With their breathing even, they pressed forward with their toes and lifted into the Reverse Triangle. Lifting their shoulders from the floor, they shifted their weight forward onto their palms and slowly raised each leg. Twisting the left leg around to rest on the right elbow, they stretched the right leg backward, high in the air.

"Hold for five, four, three, two, one, and then slowly reverse," Wilson instructed in a sexy, British accent using a deep, calming voice. "Good. I think we're ready for a bit of gatka."

Getting to her feet, Meg waited for him to grab a pair of two-foot long, wooden sticks. A type of close-range combat that originated in South Asia, gatka was a safe training method for learning otherwise dangerous weapons. The sticks simulated short swords and were meant to help perfect fighting rather than be used purely as defensive tools like many other stickfighting methods.

When they were both armed, they began. Proper footwork and tactical body positioning were key to establishing an advantage before landing a perfect blow. One-part traditional sword fight, one-part martial arts, and one-part rhythmic movement that was almost like a dance, the sport provided a cardio workout in addition to quickening reflexes and clearing the mind. The intense concentration necessary to parry strikes and set up hits in one, fluid swoop gave its practitioner a type of spiritual enlightenment that both drained and invigorated the body.

Clank. Twop. Swoosh. Pang. Shuffle. Clink. Whack.

The sounds of wood-on-wood contact echoed through the room, accompanied only by the duo's measured breathing and bare footsteps.

Wilson advanced with a one-two strike, but Meg deflected. It was then her turn to attack, spinning on her axis to set up a new position for the perfect blow. They continued until sweat dripped from both their faces and Meg's arm began to feel like it was made of rubber rather than flesh and bone.

A high hit from the six-foot three man took her out of balance, and Meg stumbled backward before landing on the floor.

Crouching next to her, Wilson extended his arm to help Meg up. "You've done well, but I think that should do it for today."

She couldn't have agreed more. It was time to end the workout, but Meg had no intention of leaving. With her pulse racing, she grabbed Wilson's hand, but Meg pulled him on top of her instead of using it to stand. Harnessing the momentum, she rolled their bodies on the floor until she was above. Sitting up, she straddled his bare torso and bent down so that her face was just inches above his.

This wasn't their first time in this position, and Wilson didn't need further encouragement. Grabbing her by the back of the head, he pulled Meg into him until his lips covered hers.

Meg left Wilson on the training room floor, still naked and dripping with even more sweat than before they began. Jumping in for a quick shower, she'd just turned on the warm stream of water when SAL buzzed in through the closed-circuit communications system. "Agent Capulet, I have a phone call for you. It's your mother, and she insist it's urgent."

Meg sat on the outdoor terrace of the Sculpture Garden's Pavilion Cafe, tapping her fingers on the wrought-iron tabletop. It was one of her favorite places in the city - just steps from the National Gallery of Art and filled with awesome displays like a Roy Lichtenstein optical illusion or The Thinker featuring a bronze rabbit instead of a man - but today she wouldn't get to enjoy any of that. Today, she was waiting to meet her mother for lunch.

Barb Brandon was a tenured professor with her summers completely free and for whom not having seen her daughter for a week constituted an emergency.

"I got you a Caesar salad," Meg said, pushing the plastic container across the table as soon as her mother arrived. She loved the woman just like any child would love a parent, but that was no reason to extend the meeting. There was also the issue of laundry and packing. Her flight for Europe left in six hours, and she was wholly unprepared.

"I had one of those for brunch yesterday, but I suppose eating the same thing two days in a row won't kill me." Barb sat and made herself comfortable. Wearing white Capri pants, a flowing yellow top, and oversized turquoise sunglasses, she looked more ready for the beach than in downtown DC.

Meg took a sip of her icy lemonade to keep herself from saying something she shouldn't. "How are you, Mom?" she asked instead.

"Regretting not having accepted my cousin's invitation to use her cabin in Yellowstone." Barb sighed, opening the lid to her meal. "I only stayed in town because I thought I could spend more time with

my daughter before the fall semester began, but we both know that's not going to happen."

"Sorry, but I told you I'd be busy." Meg scooped a bit of tuna on a cracker and popped it into her mouth. Barb knew that she never promised to make plans with her mother. That, however, still didn't stop her from attempting a good, old motherly guilt trip.

Barb used her plastic fork to mix the chopped leaves together with the grated Parmesan. "Viola Foster's daughter Suzie took her to Dollywood."

Ah, Viola Foster. The university's history department chair and Barb Brandon's social arch-nemesis. Whatever Professor Foster did, Barb wanted to out-do three-fold. And now that Viola's daughter apparently took her mother to the greatest family vacation destination in the Smoky

Mountains, Meg was expected to step up her game on the 'hanging out with mommy' front.

But as an agent at CANDY who had to be ready to go on a mission at a moment's notice, Meg's life didn't work that way. How awkward would it have been if Barb had planned to join her on vacation in Greece? With the Macedonia assignment now pre-empting her downtime, she'd have to scramble for excuses and explanations.

No, leaving her mother out of her life right now as much as possible was her only option.

"Dollywood? Really?" Meg asked in an attempt to downplay Suzie Foster's good deeds. "Isn't that the place that doesn't serve alcohol?"

Barb stopped pushing chunks of lettuce from one part of the container to the other. "Is it?" The corners of her lips slowly curled upward. "I wonder where Viola will be getting her afternoon G&Ts?"

Meg took a deep breath. Maybe that was enough for her mother to see that the grass wasn't always greener on the neighbor's lawn - or during a colleague's vacation, as it were. And although she'd thwarted the 'you're always too busy for your dear mother' conversation, Meg wasn't quick enough to stop Barb's second-most favorite line of questioning.

"Are you seeing anyone new, darling?" the older woman asked, putting her fork down and closing her salad box. She hadn't taken one bite.

Meg finished chewing another cracker and swallowed. Wiping the corner of her mouth with a paper napkin, she put on her best poker face and shook her head. "No." It wasn't untrue; she'd only had sex with two men in three days. She wasn't seeing anyone.

"Well, that's a shame. Janet Keminsky's daughter Ellen just got engaged, you know." Barb reached for her glass and drew a finger down the side to dispel the condensation. "He's a fire captain in Boston, I think."

"Ah-huh. You told me last week," Meg said, forcing herself to keep her voice even. She should have known that lunch was just her mother's covert way of wearing her down to get married and have babies. "I don't have time for a relationship at the moment."

"Yes, yes. You're focused on your career." Barb waved her hands in the air as if a career was an abstract concept. "How is work is going? Or is that another thing I can no longer ask about?"

There it was. The final nail in Meg's 'you're too good for your own mother's coffin. Spending time together, settling down with a nice boy, and talking about her job was the trifecta in the matriarchal arsenal of guilt, especially if she was reluctant to do none of it.

"Work's fine," she admitted truthfully, albeit vaguely. "I'll be away for a few weeks again starting tomorrow, though."

Barb's eyes widened. "Oh?"

"Congressman Wilde is doing some goodwill building through his position in the Committee on Foreign Relations in the Balkans, and I have to go along," Meg lied the way she was taught at CANDY: embellishing facts in a way that distorted the parts you didn't want to reveal.

It had worked so far. Her mother had never caught her in a lie.

Thanks to Meg, Barb successfully believed her daughter was a staffer for a junior member of the US House of Representatives. In fact, Jack Wilde did not exist. He was a fictitious character made up by CANDY to serve as a cover for many of their agents. Although seemingly far-fetched, the ruse had worked for over fifty years. Most Americans couldn't have been bothered enough to know who represented them in government, while the media believed anything put in front of them.

"I guess I should be happy that you're getting some sort of vacation." Barb reached over and tapped Meg's hand just as an alarm buzzed from her purse. Pulling out her smartphone, she checked the notification.

"Oh, goodness. I'd completely forgotten about this book signing I wanted to attend at Politics and Prose. You don't mind, do you?"

Mind? Meg was ecstatic to end the awkward catch-up early. "Of course, not. Go ahead."

Barb stood and kissed her daughter on both cheeks. "Call or email or at least text me while you're out of town just so I know you're all right."

Meg nodded and smiled. When her mother had gone, she grabbed her purse from the back of the chair and sat again. In the few seconds it took her to do so, a man dressed in all black slid into the opposite seat.

"You do not say anything, Miss Capulet," he said in a strong Eastern European accent. "Just listen."

Meg froze, her hand still on her bag's zipper as it stood halfway open. Of course, she was going to listen. He was using her Yard code name, for god's sake.

"The trip you are taking? From your perspective, you must fail. You understand?"

No, she didn't, and Meg shook her head.

The man leaned forward and clenched his fingers together on top of the table. "Your mission to locate

Duchess Astrid must not succeed because if it does, then your mother," he nodded in the direction Barb had just gone. "She will be dead when you return."

This time, he didn't wait for her confirmation or further questions. Pushing back the chair, the man turned, stuck his hands in his pockets, and strolled away.

For a brief moment, Meg remained still. If they - whoever they were - knew about her mother, then her identity had been compromised. Worse yet, details of her mission had leaked.

Although she felt like throwing up, Meg finished unzipping her bag, pulled out her smartphone, and typed into her encrypted message app. Agent Finn.

Copy. Go ahead. Within seconds, the answer appeared.

Lowering the device, Meg thought about the best way to phrase the situation. There really wasn't one, so she kept it short and direct: We have a problem.

Megara Ruth Brandon didn't have the type of problems that most people usually had. With all her personal information being unlisted and having a nonexistent social media presence, former classmates never invited her to tedious baby showers, wacky essential oil demos, or insufferable Fourth of July cookouts. And this was definitely fine by her.

Thanks to CANDY, Meg instead got the VIP treatment at Comic Con, and Queen Bey concerts without having to get up at two in the morning to stand in a virtual line along with ten thousand other fans hoping to grab a ticket. She also wasn't tied to a desk and was basically her own boss most of the time. But the travel perks were definitely the best part of her job.

Sure, she spent at least two hundred nights a year away from her own bed, and bad guys sometimes shot at her, but at least she got to see Antarctica in April, Lapland in September, and the Galapagos in January. She also no longer had to deal with TSA assholes who reveled in "accidentally" touching a boob during a security check. What people who were given a little power thought they could get away with was mind boggling.

Yeah, Meg didn't miss her pre-CANDY life at all. But her mother being threatened by a Slavic thug? That was definitely a new type of threat. And how did an undercover secret agent make sure that her closest relative stayed safe while she was on an international mission?

Take her along, of course!

So, with just a couple of hours left before wheels-up time, Meg convinced Barb that, in fact, she had always meant to take her on a mother-daughter work trip to the Balkans, and all that nonsense during their lunch date was just to make the ultimate revelation even grander.

"Surprise!" she had exclaimed with fake enthusiasm after catching up with Barb on the corner of Ninth and Constitution Avenue immediately following a quick chat with Finn about the unexpected wrinkle. "You didn't think I was serious, did you?" Meg asked her stupefied mother. "Of course, I'm not going on this trip alone. You're coming, too."

Barb blinked in confusion, but with that, it was settled.

Nine hours later, their C-130 turboprop transporter that had departed Joint Base Andrews with five crewmembers, eighty combat troops, and the two Brandon women landed at Alexander the Great International Airport in Skopje. Only the latter disembarked, while the rest headed toward the latest active warzone in the Middle East.

"Does that hotshot boss of yours always make you fly so . . . humbly?" Barb asked, struggling with her rolling luggage on the uneven tarmac.

Walking up front with much more purpose and grace, Meg rolled her eyes. She knew that the question—and others just like it—would come as soon as they disembarked. The Hercules wasn't made for luxury. Thanks to the greater than usual cabin noise, regular conversation wasn't practical even when their military travel-mates weren't busting into enthusiastic a capella renditions of "Old Town Road." But she could only delay for so long and now had to do what she did best: lie.

"Of course, not. But Congressman Wilde is here in a diplomatic capacity and snagging a couple of seats on a military transport is often the most cost-effective way to go," Meg said, building on her lie.

Barb laughed. "As if the US government cares about saving money."

Meg sighed, but she failed at a more appropriate comeback.

It was funny how with anyone else she always knew what to say, whether it consisted of dry sarcasm, witty banter, or straight up factual rebuttal. But with her mother—the person she'd known the longest and arguably the best—words often eluded her.

Thankfully, she was on a mission and the clock was ticking for her to dwell too long on unresolved mommy issues.

Taking a quick visual assessment of their surroundings, she noted the utilitarian glass and concrete terminal building ahead while recalling the top-secret information in her departure brief. If she was right—and she usually was—then they needed to go ....

"This way," Meg said, finding her mark and dragging Barb away from the gaggle of passengers from a just arrived commercial flight heading into the building.

"But it says 'Passport Control' right there," Barb objected, waving at the large, multilingual sign looming above a now increasingly faraway doorway.

Meg grinned at the opportunity to impress her mother. "I have a better idea."

Speeding up her steps, she took a sharp right along the back of the terminal before gently bumping into a local official standing guard at corner. The burly man slipped a bulky envelope into Meg's hand in a swift movement that was too smooth for even Barb to notice.

"Are you sure this is the right way, sweetheart?" asked the oblivious Barb as they walked toward a row of parked cars. Only a chain link fence separated the area from Skopje proper.

Meg produced a key fob, ignoring her mother while ripping the envelope open. As she aimed it at the assortment of Audis, BMWs and Mercedes, a white sedan on the end clicked to attention.

"Son of a bitch!" Meg exclaimed, eyeing the boxy piece of Russian manufacturing that should have died with the demise of the Soviet Union.

"Megara!" Barb scolded. "I hope you don't use language like that around the Congressman."

"The who?" Meg asked absentmindedly, already thinking about how to get back at Agent Finn for finding her such a pathetic ride as she reluctantly headed toward the Lada. She'd been dying to drive the new S-class Mercedes, and he gives her a forty-year-old clunker? That misstep will definitely deserve at least a clever piece of malware on his private network.

"Your boss, Megara," Barb said, idling over to the passenger side and trying the handle. "It's stuck, honey. Can you ...?" she trailed off and waved her hand at the side window instead.

Meg sighed again and got into the driver's seat. Leaning over, she tried opening the passenger door from the inside. The first tug was fruitless, but the heavy door swung open after a couple of shakes of the metal handle.

How embarrassing. She could have killed Finn for this.

After throwing their bags in the back seat, Meg started the engine. The sound could have only been compared to an old water heater that was on its last legs.

No, death was too good of punishment for Finn. He deserved slow and painful torture.

Pulling out of the parking spot, Meg headed toward the closest visible exit. A small guard's station stood next to more of the chain-link fencing. After coming to a stop at the lowered gate rail, Meg grabbed the envelope again and pulled out a wad of cash before handing it to the uniformed guard. He took it without a word, returning to his hut to raise the barrier.

"That's it? He didn't need to see our passports? Don't I get a stamp or something?" Barb asked in quick succession, craning her neck backward to look at the guard now in the distance as Meg sped away.

"Nope. That was the diplomatic exit," she said, trying to keep a straight face.

"Oh," Barb exhaled.

With their first obstacle out of the way, Meg took the adjacent roadway following a sign toward

'City Centre.' The sparse houses soon turned into bigger and denser buildings as they headed into the Paris want-to-be, post-Soviet chic with a dash of Istanbul city of Skopje.

"What's with all of the statues?" Barb asked as the urban scenery whizzed by.

Meg slowed before gunning it into a roundabout. "I dunno. You can ask the concierge. We're almost at the hotel anyway. I'll drop you off and—"

"What do you mean drop me off? You don't intend to abandon me all by myself in a foreign country just minutes after we arrive?" Barb asked, laying on the guilt as effortlessly as though she hadn't just travelled across half a dozen time zones.

Meg clenched her jaw to hold back her preferred response and took a few calming breaths. "I just thought you could relax a little bit, maybe check out the spa, and then later we can go visit the Mother Theresa Museum," she said, hoping that confinement to the hotel would keep her mother safe from would be assassins.

"Why would we do that?" Barb asked, pulling her brows together with genuine perplexity.

"Because she was born here and—," Meg repeated part of what she'd learned from her country on-board session but cut off. Her agnostic, art history professor mother obviously couldn't care less about the childhood of a famous missionary. Maybe if she mentioned the statistics regarding the insane amount of tobacco and heroin the country produced . . ..

Meg shook her head. "Never mind," she said. "I hear there is some great gold shopping, too."

"Ooh, well, that doesn't sound too bad," Barb agreed just as Meg's phone buzzed.

After quickly entering and just as aggressively exiting another traffic circle, Meg picked up the device, read the incoming text, and hit 'delete' before coming to the next intersection.

"Pick me up something pretty," she said to her mother with a smile as they pulled into the drop-off zone of the Hotel Intercontinental.

Barb waved off the porter who'd immediately jumped to open her door. "You're still not coming with me, then?" she asked, pursing her lips into a disapproving scowl.

Meg shook her phone in emphasis. "Can't. Just got word that I'm needed at work," she said, feigning regret.

"At the St. John the Baptist monastery?" Barb asked, puckering with greater ferocity.

Meg gasped. "How did you—?"

Her mother laughed. "I read the screen when you were so recklessly changing lanes."

Meg took a deep breath and turned away. Looking out the driver's side window, she contemplated her options. It didn't take long since she didn't have many. And judging by her mother's frighteningly good ability to access top-secret information, she probably couldn't be trusted to be left alone.

"Fine," Meg said grudgingly. "I'll take you with me to the monastery. But stay out of my way, okay? I've got work to do."

"You're not wearing that, are you?" Barb asked after Meg parked the car and began making preparations to walk the rest of the way to their destination.

Meg looked down at herself. The black leggings, fitted tee shirt, loose scarf, and slip-on athletic shoes were

not only super comfortable for the long flight here but also ideal to stealthily slip into and explore a medieval orthodox monastery for signs of a kidnapped heiress. Yes, she was absolutely planning on wearing it.

"Why?" she asked in return. "What's wrong with my clothes?"

Her mother shrugged. "Nothing, really. And I'll certainly leave the decision up to you," she said in a way that made it clear that she meant the opposite. "But you are a young, ambitious woman working for a powerful government official, so I would have expected you to dress a little more appropriately when acting in a business capacity."

Meg huffed. She should have figured out a way to keep her mother safe without bringing her along, preferably back in DC. But it was too late for that now.

"This is hardly an opportunity for showing off, Mom. I'm just part of the advanced team—actually, I'm THE advance team—here to scout the place out," she said one hundred percent truthfully. Sometimes describing her work for CANDY in a way that sounded almost mundane was surprisingly easy. But because Barb was still looking at her, she felt compelled to continue. "You know, to figure out where the stage should go and stuff like that in preparation for the Congressman's speech tomorrow."

"Well, that still sounds pretty important to me, but you know best," Barb said with forced resignation as she turned away.

Meg sighed. "Fine. But how am I supposed to change clothes on the side of the road?"

Barb opened the passenger and back doors. "Stand between here, and I'll keep a lookout."

After taking off the messenger bag she'd already thrown over her head, Meg grabbed a few things from her carry-on. With her mother standing guard over her modesty, she switched out the tee for a loose jersey dress and her kicks for platform boots.

Finishing off the look with a nearly invisible earpiece and a chunky bracelet for communicating with Agent Finn, she stepped away from the car and spread her arms.

"Better?" she asked, twirling around.

Barb nodded with a smile. "Much. Now, does this monastery have a buffet? Because I am parched."

Maybe you should have stayed in the hotel then; Meg thought the response she was too polite to say out loud. Instead, she secured her bag again, locked up the car, and began walking.

The thousand-year-old monastery stood on top of a hill at the end of a dirt road surrounded by miles of nothing but wheat and sunflower fields.

"So, I'm reading that most of the original structure was destroyed over the centuries, most recently in a fire in 2009," Barb said from behind.

When Meg glanced back, she saw that her mother had her nose buried in her cell phone.

"Can you turn that off, please?" she asked, thinking of all the ways anyone with a kernel of tech knowledge could ping the device. The last thing she needed was for her position to be given away to potential bad guys.

But Barb scoffed. "Absolutely not! You do remember that I'm an art historian, Megara. And from my quick research, I see that while much of the structure is reproductions, there are many priceless relics, icons, and other local treasures that I need to see."

Meg rolled her eyes. At this rate, she'd need surgery to keep them from perpetually being in a rolling state. "Right," she said. "Can you at least turn it to silent mode? Respect for the monks and all."

While Barb didn't dispute this, it didn't take her long to find something she did.

"The entry gate is this way, honey. Why are you going off that way?" she asked after Meg left the worn path and trudged into the wheat field.

Because saying that she didn't want anyone to know of their arrival wasn't an option, Meg had to come up with a believable alternative. Again.

"Uhm, one of the things I have to check for the Congressman is how good the security is in the compound so I thought we'd start with that," she said.

"By scaling the walls?" Barb deadpanned.

"No," Meg replied, eyeing the stone fagade as it ran past the fields and turned into the side of the mountain. There had to be a hidden side entrance somewhere. "By finding vulnerabilities."

No matter how right she thought she was, Meg needed help. But she couldn't get it with her mother being on her heels.

"Mom, stand over here," she said, waiving Barb over to the wall. "Stay in the shade for a minute, and don't move. I'll be right back."

Not waiting for an answer—which would have likely been an argument, anyway—Meg rounded the corner. When she was out of earshot, she activated the tech in her bracelet, bringing up a digital map. At the same time, the device in her ear also pinged to life.

"Good afternoon, Agent Capulet," Finn said cheerily from the other end. "How can I help you today?"

"Give me a way into this place, Finn," Meg said as she searched for a door.

"Copy that. Did Barb settle in okay at the InterCon?" he asked as his fingers clicked on a keyboard.

Meg looked up at the sky as though she was inspecting something. In reality, she was trying to hide her embarrassment from the upcoming answer. "Uhm, about that. Well . . . she's kind of actually here?"

The typing sound on the other end of the connection abruptly stopped. "She's what?"

Meg didn't respond.

"Agent Capulet, are you there?" Finn asked with rising agitation. "I need you to repeat what you just said, over."

"My mother is on the mission with me, all right?!"

Meg blurted out in frustration louder than she'd meant to. Looking around to make sure she hadn't been heard, she lowered her voice again. "Which is why I need to get inside as inconspicuously as possible, so can you do that for me, Finn?"

"Copy that," he replied in his usual monotone as the keyboard sounds resumed. After a few seconds, a surprised gasp rang through the connection. "I may have found something."

With her attention back on the mission's objective again, Meg touched her earpiece. Not that it did anything. "Oh, yeah? Tell me."

"The north wall looks like it runs straight into the mountain face, correct?" Finn asked.

Meg nodded as her gaze followed the structure in front of her. "Affirmative."

"Good. Now look more carefully," Finn instructed, the bubbling excitement in his voice unmistakable.

"About ten feet from the corner on the side of the rock my telemetry is showing a change in density on the vertical surface that's just about the size of a standard door. See anything that could be hiding a concealed entrance anywhere?"

Stepping closer to the area in question, Meg had no trouble finding the possible spot for a secret door. Out of the entire vicinity, only one patch of the rock face was covered with a swatch of dense ivy.

"Bingo-"

"Is everything all right over here?" Barb interrupted just as Meg declared victory.

She spun around, feeling as though she'd been caught with her hand in a cookie jar. "Mom? I thought I told you to stay put."

"Well, you were taking so long and—"

Meg gave in despite having no time to argue and even less of a willingness to do so. "Never mind. No worries. And look," she pointed to the mass of climbing vines. "I found what I was looking for."

As her mother mumbled something about it looking like it was more trouble than it was worth, Meg reached into her bag and pulled out a switchblade.

The sharp weapon easily cut through the ivy, quickly revealing an ancient door hidden for who knows how long. Wedging the blade between the jamb and the lock, Meg popped open the door in one swift motion.

A waft of cool, musty air hit her face, but the darkness and quiet emanating from the hallway indicated that it was—at least for now—deserted. Exchanging the knife for a flashlight, Meg waved to her mother as she stepped inside. "Follow me."

Too bad she didn't see the body lying in her path.

A good spy always needed to be aware of three things: the passage of time, the viability of escape routes, and the presence of dead bodies. Meg had definitely failed at least on one of those counts in that moment.

As her center of gravity pulled her forward in the dank tunnel, Meg's outstretched hand collided against the wall, but at least it prevented her from taking an even nastier fall. "Son of a bitch!" she exclaimed as the rough stone scraped up the skin of her palm before shining the flashlight's beam down to examine the unforeseen obstacle.

Tiny particles of dust floated in the air as the unusual scene came into view. The term 'dead body' was an understatement. Judging by the tattered rags hanging off the desiccated skeleton, the unfortunate soul who had met their demise in the basement of the monastery had been there for decades, if not centuries.

In a humorously delayed reaction, Barb screamed.

"Stay quiet, will you?" Meg shushed her mother before kicking a shinbone out of the way. "It's obviously fake, leftover from a spooky tour or something."

Barb huddled closer to her daughter, squeezing Meg's shoulders from behind. "Are you sure?"

Meg held back a laugh at the realization that it took a trip halfway across the world to find her mother's weakness. "Positive," she lied. "Now, let's keep moving. At this rate, we'll be spending eternity down here, too."

The windowless tunnel also had no offshoots, no turns, and no way out other than a single door at the far end. Although it lacked a locking mechanism, it wouldn't budge no matter how hard Meg pushed down on the handle.

"Stand back," she instructed, waving her mother away. Raising her foot, she kicked the wooden panel at just the right spot before it flew open. And while she had expected criticism for her aggressive method, she got instead a fifty-year-old art historian blow past her like a mini tornado.

True to form, Barb didn't dwell long on her momentary panic, but used her well-tested methods of steering the conversation her way. "Oh, goodness. Look at this place. And you wanted me to stay behind," she said, trying to keep her ragged breathing even as she reveled in the sight of where they'd emerged.

Meg followed her out, her eyes squinting at the brightness. It wasn't just from extra light. The domed room was full of bling: golden mosaics from wall to ceiling, gilded trims, and sparkly silver accessories. The Medieval chapel was a venerable Mecca for an art historian, and Meg breathed a sigh of relief. It looked to be the perfect spot to park her mother while she scoped out the rest of the compound.

"Dive in, Mom," she said after making sure there weren't any baddies hiding in the dark corners. "The place is yours. Just don't break anything. I'll be back when I'm done with work."

"All right, honey," Barb said absentmindedly as she picked up the bejeweled chalice in the middle of the altar and flipped it upside down as if she were looking for a price tag.

As Meg slipped out the front, she pulled the wrought-iron key from inside and used it to lock the door from the outside. Unless someone used the same secret tunnel they'd entered through, her mother would be safe and sound until her return. Judging by the spacious layout of the numerous buildings surrounding the courtyard where she stood, that could take quite a while.

Tapping on her comms device, Meg checked in.

"Agent Finn, do you copy?"

"He's currently unavailable, Agent Capulet," SAL's measured reply came at once. "I will be assisting you in the meantime."

Meg shrugged. Although she'd never been handed off to the AI during a mission, SAL had always proven to be a valuable asset, and she was sure she'd be in good hands.

"Very well, SAL. Please give me a thermal read of the monastery grounds. Over."

"Besides you, there is one other person in the facility based on body temperature," SAL said.

Meg furrowed her brows. She knew that the place was officially closed for renovations and that the monks had temporarily moved to another location. But based on intelligence from CANDY, she'd been expecting to find the people behind Astrid Louisa von Alsace- Thuringen's kidnapping if not the Duchess' herself here. The single readout beside her own belonged to her mother, meaning that they were alone.

And that didn't feel right.

Taking as much care to stay silent and invisible, Meg drew a handgun from her bag. She hugged the walls as she proceeded to clear each room and building in an established matrix pattern. This wasn't the time to go rogue or rush. Thankfully, it seemed like she had the luxury of both time and access.

The layout and contents of the monastery appeared straightforward. The public spaces had places for worship, contemplation, and gathering. There was even a ubiquitous gift shop selling trinkets and souvenirs. After leaving a crisp bill on the counter, Meg slipped a refrigerator magnet replica of the place into her pocket.

The private areas also started off uneventful. Dormitories with multiple beds in each served as the monks' residence, while an industrial kitchen connected to an obvious dining room. But then there was the hall of weirdness.

That was the only way Meg could mentally describe the large room adjacent to the well-stocked library. It was the only room she'd found locked so far, although a well-placed bullet solved that obstacle. Electric faux-candles lit wall sconces inside the windowless space, already ratcheting up the creepy factor. But then came the artifacts.

With some resting in glass display cases and others just hanging on the walls, the increasing stranger and stranger items quickly monopolized Meg's attention. There were swords, daggers, crossbows, stakes, maces, and muskets. Although these were a bit unusual for the ascetic location, they weren't too out of the ordinary for a serious collector of antique weapons.

The assortment of stuffed werewolves was another story.

The taxidermied lycanthropes mostly stood on their hind legs in all of their furry glory. With clawed hands reaching for the sky and teeth bared, they loomed over Meg as she walked by. A few were displayed on all-fours, mimicking a sort of gallop, and one unfortunate specimen only had the chance to have his severed head mounted on the wall.

"What the hell?" Meg whispered as she examined the realistic fur on a russet beast. The craftsmanship was marvelous, and if she hadn't been positive that werewolves weren't just the stuff of legends, she might have believed that these were actually real.

The bang of the door as it flew open interrupted her musings. In the opening, two masked strangers, clad all in black, stood ready in a fighting position.

"Hey SAL," she called to the high-tech assistant. "I thought you said there weren't any other people here."

"That's correct, Agent Capulet," the artificial voice confirmed with an over-the-top cheer.

Meg cocked her gun. "Then who are these guys that just showed up?" she asked frantically before barrel rolling for cover.

A bullet struck the display case, shattering the glass before raining its shards over Meg's head. Squeezing her eyes shut, she ducked further down and waited for the spray of rounds to lull. When her attackers seemed to be reloading, she took her chance.

Standing up, she aimed in the direction she thought they were and pulled the trigger. The two in black, however, were both quick and clever. This definitely wasn't their first take-out. Running ahead of the lethal ordnance, they split up and found cover before any of the rounds found their marks.

"Dammit," Meg whispered, lowering her weapon and crouching back down. But she didn't have a chance to catch her breath.

As she checked how many shots she had left, footsteps approached from the right. Spinning around, she was just in time to dodge a well-placed right hook. She also prepared to strike in one swift motion, hitting the masked attacker in the gut.

The attacker recoiled, but only to grab the medieval mace from the shattered display. Rotating the spiked ball with a flick of his wrist in a figure-eight position, they slowly advanced as Meg crab-walked backward. When her shoulders hit something not quite sturdy, she knew she'd found the second assailant. Extending her right leg, she swung around and swept him off his feet before he had a chance to react. This gave her a chance to jump up and once again take aim. The single shot hit the mace-wielding attacker in the shoulder before ricocheting off with a loud "ping."

They had thermal scrambling body-suits, and the gear was also highly bulletproof. Cool, she thought to herself with a heavy dollop of sarcasm. Maybe my runway boots can fly me out of here.

Bam.

The kick to the middle of her back brought Meg back to reality. Catching herself with the help of a stuffed wolfman, she avoided eating the ground, but probably not a cracked rib or two by the feel of it. After righting herself, she tilted her head to one side and then to the other to crack her neck.

"Oh, you wanna play?" she asked the baddies among the rubble. "Let's play."

Kick. Punch. Slam. Roll.

Swipe. Tackle. Shoot. Bite.

Evade. Push. Chop. Throw.

The trio used all moves and combinations in *Every Spy's Guide to Hand-to-Hand Combat* and still came up even. Of course, Meg was fighting two at a time, so really, she was much better than them. But she was also really, really tired of getting beaten up.

Looking to take the fight to perhaps someplace where she could have an advantage, Meg ran to the room's only door in—and out—. When she opened it, she knew she'd lost.

Because standing on the other side was Barb Brandon. If seeing her daughter in the middle of an all-out brawl with two assassins wasn't bad enough, she also had a gun aimed straight at her head.

"Mom?" Meg shrieked as she dropped her arms to her side. Wasting no time, one of the masked assailants kicked the gun out of her hand before buckling her knees from behind, forcing her to the ground.

"I'm so sorry, Megara," Barb sobbed, shaking where she stood. "I know you told me to stay put, but I got curious and—"

"Save the apologies, liebchen," said the woman keeping her in a chokehold and pointing the barrel of the dainty semi-automatic to her head. "We all know that you'll never take anything your daughter says seriously, and she'll forever keep resenting you for it."

After getting over her initial shock at the reveal and then her quick anger at the personal jab, Meg didn't need introductions to know exactly who she was dealing with. The supermodel looks, the runway-ready outfit, and the confident demeanor all pointed to the missing member of the Alsace-Thuringen family.

"Hello, Astrid," Meg said with a satisfied smirk. Somehow, she had suspected that Occam's razor had been in play during the supposed kidnapping plot.

And now, seeing that the most likely answer—in that the snatched victim was actually in cahoots with the perpetrators—was true, she could finally stop trying to unboggle the mystery.

"I have to say, I didn't think you'd reveal yourself so soon, but I'm thankful that you didn't make us follow you all over the world in a wild goose chase," she said with a lot more self-assurance than a person should have in that type of situation. "But I do have to ask. What the heck is up with all of those damn werewolf mounts in there?"

The rough gun barrel poke against the back of her head made Meg tilt forward. "Ouch."

"Should I do it now just to get her to shut up?" asked the woman who'd been one of Meg's attackers just a few minutes earlier.

Astrid took a moment to ponder. "No," she finally said as though she were just refusing a side of fries with lunch. "All that blood would be impossible to get out of the parquet floor. Let's go down to the courtyard to finish them off."

"Finish us off?" Barb screeched again as she was forced down the adjacent stairs. "What does she mean, Megara? What have you gotten us into? Where is the Congressman to help us?"

Meg sighed as she walked behind, also at the urging of a gun in her ribs. "So, there's no Congressman, Mother. And I'm not here to set up a speech about cultural heritage. It was all a lie, just like everything else I've told you about my job for the last five years."

Astrid laughed.

"Oh, you think that's funny?" Barb asked, exerting her university professor voice on the woman intent on executing her in a few minutes' time.

But it seemed to work. "No, ma'am," Astrid said, and Meg almost felt sorry for the girl.

Then she remembered how they all got into this mess.

"So, about that faked kidnapping," she said, hoping to at least get an insight on the motivations behind everything before her upcoming demise.

"Pretty genius, wouldn't you say?" Astrid asked with a laugh as they left the building and entered the deserted courtyard.

Meg shrugged. "Only if you think putting out obvious signs pointing to your jealous cousin Wiktor as the culprit while leaving a sloppy trail of being in on it counts as genius."

Astrid waved for her thugs to position Meg on her knees in front of her before setting Barb in the same style next to her. Crossing her arms while tapping her own brow with the barrel of her weapon, she smiled again.

"I don't know," she began in her posh European accent. "I think that sets everything up nicely to expose Henri as the real mastermind, using his innocent sister's naivete to frame the usurper cousin plotting for the family inheritance."

"What?" Barb asked, looking thoroughly confused. "I'm sorry, but I don't follow."

Meg nodded. "Oh, I do, and you're right, Astrid. It is quite a good plan." Turning to her mother, she gave a quick wink before continuing. "You see, Mom. Through the order of succession followed in Luxenstein, Astrid could only become Grand Duchess after both her older brother Henri and her newly discovered cousin Wiktor had somehow become ineligible. That usually means death, but jailing or public outcry can also work. So, she came up with a plan that would sully both of their names. No matter which outcome prevailed—the one where Wiktor was thought to be a ruthless kidnapper or Henri the cunning manipulator—Astrid would always be seen as the innocent victim."

Astrid clapped, the gun still dangerously waving in her hands. "Bravo. And now that we've gotten that whole Scooby Doo reveal out of the way, I think you can now die with a peace of mind."

Meg had hoped that her monologue about the intricacies of the plan would lead to something.

Whether it was a revelation about a way out, an epiphany regarding how to fight back, or just a
distraction for a rescue party that even she didn't know about didn't matter. But now she was here, kneeling on the hard-packed dirt in the middle of a monastery in Macedonia waiting for a bullet to the brain. And worse yet, her mother was in the same position right next to her.

"Can I just say something real quick?" Meg asked in a last-ditch effort to stall. Living for a moment longer was better than the alternative. Turning to her mother, she forced a smile. Telling the overbearing, stubborn, and judgmental woman just how much she meant to her wasn't going to be easy, but if it was the last chance she had.

The sound of spinning rotors came before anyone saw or felt the helicopter. When it appeared in the sky above the roofline, it was too late for Astrid and her crew to attack. A steady spray of bullets on either side of the hostage circle prevented her from fleeing, and in the melee, the young heiress forgot about shooting Meg and Barb.

As the chopper landed, it stirred up so much dirt that visibility was nearly zero until the rescue party had them surrounded. Only then did Meg recognize the man dressed in sleek combat gear with a rifle slung over his shoulder.

"Ryan?" she asked in a bewildered tone as her K Street consultant, bird enthusiast neighbor walked up and scooped her up into a grateful hug.

He squeezed her tight. "Yeah, but you can keep calling me Agent Finn, if you'd like."

"I still can't believe I didn't figure out that the voice that guided me through dozens of missions belonged to the hottie living next door," Meg said before taking a sip of her Spritz Veneziano.

On the lounger beside her, Ryan—also known as Agent Huck Finn—adjusted his sunglasses and laughed. "You can't be the only competent spy working at CANDY, can you?"

Meg turned and looked him up and down. Six foot two ripped as hell, and having a face that belonged on a Times Square billboard advertising expensive cologne. Sigh. He was absolutely perfect.

"Tell me again how you saved us," she said with an exaggerated bat of her eyelashes before sucking on the straw again to drink the fizzy concoction.

Ryan shifted his weight, and the sunchair sank deeper into the soft, Hellenic sand. "How many times do you need to hear that boring story?" he asked in his perfectly British accent.

Meg patted his arm, the tanned skin warm under her touch. "It's not boring. Now, go on."

He sighed. "Fine, but this time I'm going to give all the credit to SAL because, without them, you and Barb would . . .." He trailed off as his expression sank at the thought of the alternative outcome.

After clearing his throat, Ryan continued. "Anyway, since that device on your wrist is basically a glorified FitBit, SAL—as you know—was listening in to everything that happened after you were attacked. But what was even more crucial is that they had calculated the probability of an ambush even before you had touched down in

Macedonia, so by the time you entered the monastery, I had gotten my orders to break cover to enter as backup."

"Wait," Meg interjected. "You all knew that there was a high likelihood of us getting into trouble, and CANDY allowed the mission to go on? In other words, my mother and I were used as bait?" The realization, which should have long been obvious, had just occurred to her.

Ryan's face went red. "Uhm, well . . .. There are certain protocols—"

Meg shook her head and waved him off. "Forget it. My anger is misdirected, I'm sure. I'll speak with Stoker when we're back in DC. Continue the story."

"As I was saying, SAL then took over my usual duties of assisting you remotely while I hopped on the chopper and waited just outside the walls to step in at the right moment."

"Good thing, too. Imagine if you'd have been back at HQ thousands of miles away like you usually are when I'm on a mission."

Ryan grimaced. "About that . . .."

Meg's eyes widened. "You're kidding! If you're not directing me from HQ, then where?"

"I'm usually pretty close," Ryan admitted. "Always in-country, sometimes just a few miles away. Occasionally within the same building."

Meg pouted. Son of a bitch. Her intelligent wingman was on her tail, and she'd never even noticed. In fact, she'd done many things to accomplish her objectives just because she didn't think anyone was truly listening. No one really mattered, at any rate.

"Madrid?" she asked.
"Across the street."
"Shanghai?"
"Upstairs."
"Bogota?"
"In the room next door."

Her heart sank. While five minutes ago Meg had thought she could have a more-than-friends relationship with this guy, now she wasn't so sure. He'd heard her have sex with marks for god's sake!

"Megara, are you okay?" Ryan asked, swinging his long legs over the lounger as he sat up.

She mirrored his stance and put her hands on his knees. Switching into professional spy-mode, she shut out her emotions. "Yeah. Of course," she lied before standing. "Let's go for a swim. We're not in Mykonos every day, now, are we?"

But Ryan grabbed her hand before she had a chance to leave. His rock-hard body pressed against hers as he stood up, their swimsuits the only pieces of clothing separating them. "I've never listened in when I shouldn't have, if that's what you're worried about," he whispered, their noses just millimeters apart.

"You haven't?" Meg asked weakly, realizing the implications of his confession.

He shook his head. "Nope. Couldn't bear it, if I had," Ryan said before his lips clamped down on hers.

The End

OTHER BOOKS BY THE AUTHOR

Karmic Love

Undercover

Eternal Love

Undying Lust

The Good Taste

Offence and Justice

A Model for Murder

Lethal Legacy

Lethal Legacy 2

Paranormal Club

Enchanted Souls

Beginners of Nowhere

Wildflower

Mystic Agent

Dark Angel

Lonesome Moonlight

The Eerie Egg

A Romantic Crime .

Passionate Alien

Dragon Knight

The Critical Case

In the Shadow

Mental Asylum

Athena